A Kitten Named,

"*Little Rip*"

A Halloween Tale Inspired by a True Story!

By Don Claybrook, Ph.D.

Illustrated by Meili Daniel

AuthorHouse™
1663 Liberty Drive
Bloomington, IN 47403
www.authorhouse.com
Phone: 833-262-8899

Illustrated by Meili Daniel

ISBN: 978-1-6655-3728-5 (sc)
ISBN: 978-1-6655-3729-2 (e)

Library of Congress Control Number: 2021918393

Print information available on the last page.

Published by AuthorHouse 09/14/2021

authorHOUSE

Dedication

This book is specifically about two of my children, Autumn Claire (Claybrook) Kriofske, Seattle; (Autumn in the book) and, Donald Adrian Claybrook, Jr., Stallion Springs, California (Donny in the book). In addition to these two, the book is dedicated to all four of my children which also includes Landa Patrice (Claybrook) Boutte, Corpus Christi Texas and Liberty Jackson Claybrook-Reyes, AKA, *"Jack,"* Kerrville Texas.

I also dedicate this book to two of the finest people I've ever known, Jerry and Brenda Ledford of Georgetown Indiana, faithful members of Georgetown Baptist Church where I pastored during the time of this inspired Halloween story. It was in Georgian Acres, a safe community where they lived, that we always took our kids *Trick-or-Treating*, and theirs, three of my favorites, Lori, Tammy and Greg, along with my middle two, Autumn and Donny, who, along with *"Little Rip,"* are the subjects of our story.

Finally, I dedicate this children's book to all the children in the seven churches I've pastored over the years. Those would be, in this order, First Baptist Church, Redwood Valley California, 1975-77; First Baptist Church of Cloverdale California, 1977-78; Georgetown Baptist Church, Georgetown Indiana, 1978-83; Rolling Fields Baptist Church, Jeffersonville Indiana, 1983-1987; South Park Baptist Church, Beaumont Texas, 1987-1990; Mendocino Baptist Church, Mendocino California, 1996-2000; and Interim pastor at Greenwood Community Church, Elk California, 2005-2007. And to the good people at Mendocino Presbyterian Church in Mendocino California where I am presently a member and facilitator/teacher of the co-ed adult Sunday School class.

I believe that the future of America, this land we love, is in good hands…with my four children and my four grandchildren, along with all those children to whom I've dedicated this Halloween Story. May you go with God and make a difference. A difference which counts toward the ushering in of a better world for your children and grandchildren. Just remember, making a difference in this world for the better is so much more important than making a fortune.

<u>Acknowledgements</u>

Photos credits to Don Claybrook, Jr. *(a professional photographer)*, and the author, Don Claybrook, Sr. unless otherwise specifically noted.

<u>Meili Daniel:</u> All other artwork and illustrations are by Meili Daniel, the daughter of my good friends, Viv and Morgan Daniel. We are all members of the Mendocino Presbyterian Church on the beautiful Mendocino Coast of Northern California. Morgan makes fine, world-renowned, custom guitars, Viv is a Health Care Professional, and Meili is a senior at Mendocino High School.

I want to take this opportunity to thank Meili. Without her contribution, this book would just be another Halloween tale. With it, I have reason to believe the book could become a *Halloween Children's Classic*! With proper and sufficient marketing, of course. It was designed to appeal to all ages, whether the one who reads it to children or the reader him/herself.

Finally, I am compelled to humbly offer acknowledgement and heart-felt gratitude to my Lord for His Amazing Grace which has brought me safe thus far, and will lead me home. With the Apostle Paul, I too can say: *"I can do ALL things through Christ who strengthens me.* And, *Without Him, I can do nothing"*…my Lord, my Savior, and my constant companion who has promised me He will never leave me, nor forsake me. Of this one thing, <u>I am sure!</u>

A Kitten Named "*Little Rip*"

By Don Claybrook, Ph.D.

Autumn was a little girl,
    Just 11-year's old.
        She was in 5th grade,
           And did as she was told….
           (Most of the time!)

        Her middle name was Claire,
          Named after her mother,
            Autumn had golden hair,
              Her dad thought Autumn Claire,
               Had a name like no other!

     She had a little brother,
        He was smart like Shirley, their mother.

But, they just called him, *"Donny."*
Donald Adrian was his name.
And for that…he had his dad to blame.
Or his granddad who gave his dad the name!
At any rate, both were named the same!
I guess two can play that game!

Donny was in 3rd grade, and 9-year's old.
Together with Autumn, they had a paper route,
The winters in Indiana can get awfully cold!
There's very little doubt, the weather,
Is what that route was all about.

COLD!
COLD!
COLD!

Autumn felt that Donny was smitten.
She thought *"I'd really like to have a kitten."*
But Mom said, *"It was nice to have a little brother."*
And Dad added, *"You might find it very hard,
Choosing one over the other."*

But Autumn just rolled her eyes and muttered under her breath,

"OH BROTHER!"

"But who knows?
    A kitten would be lovely,
        A brother a pet is not.
            I really want a kitten,
                But I guess a brother's what I've got."

"I wish I had a kitten
    Meow!
        Purr!
            Run!
                Run!
                    Run!
But all I have's a brother.
    And he's seldom much fun."

Suddenly it came to her,
        From way down deep within.

Wow! It was great!
She thought Donny would surely buy-in,
So, she shared with him her secret plan.
They could hardly wait for Halloween,
Because…her plan was allegedly grand!

They shouted and they jumped and yelled!
As they planned and planned their plan.
They plotted! And planned again.
And now they had it!!!
But then they plotted and planned again!
And again!

And oh! The plan was super-swell!
It would work perfectly well,
And simply be super-da-duper.
But then again….you never can tell.
There could be a party pooper!
With a claw hammer,
And a 10-penny nail!
Raising, all kind of…cane!
And going insane….
But only time would tell!

4

Autumn teaching Donny all about kittens, as she shares
her plan! Donny, on the other hand, invites a few
of his more intelligent friends to the lecture!

"I know Halloween's
     coming," Said Autumn,
          "And we can 'trick-or-treat',
               And it will surely work out right,
                    Because my plan's so neat."

"Now that's exactly what we'll do,"
     Autumn told her little brother.
          "And when Halloween finally comes,
               I'll share my plan more further."

"It's really a fantastic and great idea,
     And I'll soon tell the rest to you.
          And no one…but no one,
               Will know just what we'll do."
                    And that's just plain old true!

Caveat: One never knew…with those two!

"*Autumn!*" My mom was calling,
She called Donny too.
"*I wondered what she wanted,*"
My brother said, <u>*"She knew!"*</u>

"*Oh phoo, she doesn't know!*
Donny! I'm not scared a bit.
But if you dare tell Mom,
My kitten I'll never get."

Donny Just shrugged his shoulders,
As his sister thought out loud,
"*I doubt that he will tell.*"
She said, seeming awfully proud.
"*Cause when he told the last time,*
I really rang his bell!"

"Oh dear, my lovely children,"
How my mom could gush.
"You've got to do your homework."
She was always in such a rush.

The second time she called,
Donny really started to run.
Whereupon Autumn thought,
"He's sure not a kitten,
Sometimes, he's just <u>NO</u> fun!"

"Autumn, Donny!
Time to eat," Said mom
"Time to wash your hands."
She was in the kitchen,
Rattling pots and pans.
While popping her wrist with rubber bands!
And rubbing lotion on her hands.

9

Mom, Shirley Claire, busy in the kitchen

"Don't you worry," Autumn told Donny.
"She knows nothing at all."

And then they heard their dad,
Coming down the hall!
He was really frowning,
And looked like he'd been bitten.
And they wondered if he'd guessed their plan,
The plan about the kitten.
Oh yes, the kitten they were gettin.

Dad, the pastor, just getting in from his church office.

"Hello kids! Autumn, Donny.
How was your day?" Dad said.
Then he gathered them for dinner,
While humbly bowing his head,
And Autumn wishing she were dead!

Her mother was checking one of her hourglasses,
While scratching her head! Here's what she said,
"After you've eaten, do your homework,
Autumn, Donny! Are you listening?
And then go straight to bed!"

Dad asked for the Lord's forgiveness,
Because, *"Each of us is a sinner!"*
And then he thanked God,
For every last thing they had!
Plus, Forgiveness…and oh yes,
He almost forgot to thank Him for Dinner!
But…that's just Dad….
Or any preacher….I guess!
Always wanting somebody to confess!

As twilight falls, Dad thanking the Lord for everything they had...with
Autumn keeping an eye on him...and Mom *"shushing"* Donny!

"We don't have everything,"
   Thought Autumn,
     "We don't have a kitten…."
      But then dad said, *"Amen!"*
       Which all seemed rather fitten.

But Autumn moped about the kitten,
   The one that she was gettin'.
     Oh yes, the kitten she <u>hoped</u> that she was gettin.

At bedtime, Dad tucked them in bed…and,
   Autumn prayed, *"Now I lay me down to sleep…."*
     Then as she began to fade, she also began to weep!
     "Dear Lord, Dad's prayer at dinner tonight,
      Made me hurt inside….waaay down deep,
       In that 'hurting place'…and waaay out of sight!"

"But I promise, Lord, to keep on loving you!
   If you could please bring me a kitten too,
     I mean, if that's alright with you?
      In Jesus name, Amen….
       P.S. And God! Goodnight to you…too!
        Again!"

THE NEXT MORNING AS AUTUMN AWAKENS!

"Why do the days take so long?
And the nights, they're long too.
When I was just nine years old
Oh, how the time just flew!"

"I didn't even care about days or months or years,
Dad said I spent most of my time just shifting gears!
And Mom said I was just like her,
That my whole life was one big blur!
But Donny said that now all I wanted,
Was something with fur....
And it had darn sure better purr!"
"And to that, I say, "YES SIR!"

"But now that I have a plan
To get myself a kitten,
Time doesn't really move at all,
And my brother? Well,
That story's not yet been written...."

Donny, marching to the beat of a different drummer!
While Autumn ponders her now dubious decision
to share her plan to get a kitten at Halloween with him!

"Now, I know Donny's really smart!
At least, that what people say!
But he's got to do his part,
To replace our kitten, <u>"Spot"</u>
That just up and ran away!"

"He doesn't have a spot on him!"
Dad said to me one day.
"So why did I name him that?"
But I just said, "Well Dad, that's OK!
"What did you want me to say?
<u>'The Cat'?</u> No way, Jose!"

"September, and then October,"
Shirley Claire, their mom announced today.
Autumn Claire cried, "I'm waiting for October
But September's here to stay!
If October ever comes
Can Halloween be far away?"

To which Donny replied, *"Yes it can be far away! Like a whole month, mostly."*
To which Dad explained, *"He's already acting ghostly."*
Autumn just rolled her eyes and added, *"Or postly!"*

"But when Halloween finally comes," she screamed,
    "I'll
        Play!
            Play!
                Play!

And with a wink and a whisper at her little brother, said,
    "Oh Donny! I can't wait for that day!"

Dad said when it was time to *"Trick-or-Treat,"*
    We'd go to Georgian Acres.
        Said *"That's surely the safest place.*
            With nothing but 'Movers and Shakers!'
                And lots of Baptist and Quakers!"

Donny leaned over,
And whispered to Autumn,
"I really like Georgian Acres.
We go there every year.
They're the givers,
And we're the takers!
To me that's pretty clear."

"We're the takers?" Mused, a confused Autumn,
"What do you mean by that?"
Donny responded, *"What? "We go there every year?*
Or, to me that's pretty Clear?"
To which Autumn replied,
"Donny! You're just a little brat."
And their mother, in exasperation muttered, *"Ohhhh*
dear! Now just stop that!"

Halloween finally came.
Autumn thought her plan was sure,
To get herself a kitten,
All fluffy, white, and pure.

"With Donny's help," Thought Autumn,
   "This plan's just got to work,
     If he doesn't decide at the last minute,
      To be a little jerk!"

She knew just what she'd name her Kitten.
   He'd come each time she'd call.
     And they would romp and frolic,
      She'd call her kitten,

Snowball!!!

They'd laugh and run and play.
   And, that's not all,
     They'd really have a ball.

Autumn dressed up like a sweet angel.
Donny was a plain, normal? ghost.
She said, *"Come on Slowpoke! Hurry!"*
But, he just stood there like a post.
Doing what a ghost does most.
And thinking, *("This plan is toast!")*.

She shouted, *"Now what's the matter?*
You know I want a cat!"
He said, *"Autumn!*
I don't want to do it!"
And that, was that, was that!

"Oh my gosh!" Said Autumn,
"Gag me with a gnat!"
"I don't care," Said Donny.

And that,

Was that,

Was that!

<u>Autumn and Donny dressing for *Trick-or-Treat!*</u>

Autumn was so angry, she could hardly think,
There was nothing she could do.
The plan she'd planned to get her kitten,
Would, <u>certainly</u> take two.

Her brother, the ghost, just looked at her,
As they went to *"trick-or-treat."*
Autumn stared right back at him,
Wanting their eyes to meet.

But Donny turned and walked slowly away,
A ghost with little feet.

*"Forget my plan, forget my cat,
Forget my brother, the little brat.
To make a plan was really dumb.
Donny's impossible! The little bum."*

Autumn said out loud,
     As she joined the Halloween crowd,
          An angry angel heading down the street,
          "I might as well 'trick-or-treat.'"

Ring!

Ring!

Ring!

**Autumn ringing the doorbell at the Ledford's Home
in Georgian Acres.**

26

While ringing the doorbell, she pondered!
("I'm really good at ringing bells!")
Then she waited…and her mind wandered.
("If you don't believe me,") she thought,
("Ask that little ghost! And he'd better tell!")

"Well good grief and holy cow,
Where in the world is Donny now?
I saw him with those neighbor boys,
And all they were doing was making noise!"

The boys were darting this way and that,
Like drunken fireflies or a blind gnat!
And running in circles like a two-legged snail,
With the other foot held fast,
By a 10-penny nail!!!!!

"Gimme a break!" (she whispered),
Just as the Ledford's answered their bell,
(That would be Brenda, along with Jerry….
Back before the iPhone and the Blackberry!
But, I guess you could tell).

Autumn heard them opening the door!!!
("Oh, for Pete's sake! What have I wrought?
But don't give me a second thought.
Just Never mind!
But, I'll give you a little hint,
It was NOT very kind.")
She thought while panicking,
In her messed-up mind!

"We have nothing to give."
Said the Ledford's,
"We have no gum or candy."

Whereupon Autumn quietly mused,
"Now that's just dandy!
No gum?
No candy?"

"Wait!" Exclaimed Brenda,
As Autumn stood there in awful pain,
Thinking it was time she was quittin'.
Then they came right back and handed her,
A beautiful baby kitten!

Jerry explained, *"We have no gum or candy,*
Or anything like that......" Then Brenda interrupted,
"All we have is this kitten, brought home by our cat....
<u>*'Miss Scat!'"*</u>

Whereupon Jerry rolled his eyes
And sarcastically concluded,
"The last thing we needed...was another cat.
Besides, after 'Miss Scat',
Who could of ever come up
With a better name than that! For a cat?"
And that,
Was that,
Was that!
Autumn just stood there in misery,
And in all her angel gear,
And reflected...while her halo rested...on one ear,
With a sad heart, she no longer felt so tough.
"I usually get lots of candy, and other nice stuff,
When we come here every year.
But there doesn't seem to be much cheer,
This year."
Wept Autumn, through a tear.

Autumn day-dreaming about lots of candy and other nice stuff! And thinking, "ONLY ONE???"

About then the kitten started licking her,
And she was thinking, *"This is NOT real."*
Then she saw the kitten's fur.
So she stroked it….just to feel.

The kitten was so soft and nice and warm,
Its coat was smooth and black.
A white star streaked down its face,
She couldn't give it back!
So…..she put it in her sack.

"But wait!" Screamed Autumn,
    As she strolled home in the night.
      "What am I gonna call my kitten?
    It's black and not white!
        'Snowball's' just not right."

And Autumn Claire, the angel, was quite a sight,
    She and her kitten on that Halloween night.

The kitten started scratching
    And making quite a noise,
      Suddenly Autumn saw Donny,
    And all those rowdy boys.

She told them she had no candy,
    And they laughed and screamed a lot,
        But then they saw her sack
            And shouted,

"Hey Autumn, what you got?"
"Meow!" purred the kitten,
As it ripped the sack apart.
Then stuck its head through the hole,
And gave the boys a start.

33

Autumn and boys looking at her Halloween sack!

"Little Rip" Showing his disdain for the sack!

Donny cried, <u>"I want that kitten!"</u>
    With a quiver on his lip.
        Then the kitten raised its pretty head,
           Like it didn't give a flip.
                Whether it was alive or dead,
                    And, for that matter,
                        What anybody said!

Then Autumn screamed like she'd been bitten,
As she shouted at the kitten,
While relaxing her grip.
"Well you Little Rrrrriii……!
Oh my goodness… that's it!"

"Little Rip!"

"Little Rip" staring at the stunned boys!

Then she scolded Donny, *"You want <u>MY</u> kitten?"*
As *"Little Rip"* softly licked her hand.
"Where in the world were you hiding,
When it was time to do my plan?"

"You wanted to 'trick-or-treat,'
To have a lot of fun,
And now you want to share,
When all is said and done."

"Autumn," pleaded the little ghost,
"I'll split my candy with you.
And, I'll give you the most.
Which is quite a few.
Well…
More than one or two!"

So Autumn thought about it,
As Donny stood there like a post!
Then said to her little brother,

"For a 'taker' who brags a lot!
Especially for a dumb old ghost!
You're the only brother I've got,
So, I guess………..Why not?"
You're not much worse than most,
Ghost or post!

Dad taught us that the best way to show,
Following Jesus is the best way to know,
That we love Him! And love one another.

Well, I know it went something like that!
So I should love my Dad and my mother.
And oh yeah, that little ghost, my brother!

I'm pretty sure that's what Dad meant by that.
But I wonder if that includes me getting a cat?
I'd better check with my Dad on that little blip,
When I get home tonight with <u>OUR</u> kitten,"
"Little Rip."

"So...Donny...maybe I do love you.....some,
Even though you can be a little bum!
I'd say.....it's a pretty low bar,
But I guess that's what sisters are for!
At least that's what Mom and Dad said today!
And, for them, I'd say...that's about par!"

Donny, who'd been listening and pondering,
("Wow! That was quite a rambling rant!
Now, why don't you give us a rousing chant?")
But then he reflected,
"If I said that again,
It might be a sin."
So he changed his mind and took a different tack,
And talked of that which is from above!

LOVE!
Or perhaps his tack…
Was to talk a little smack!

Who knows?

"Thank you Autumn," sweetly whispered Donny,
As he snuggled *"Little Rip"* close to his chest.

"So far as I know, you're the only sister I've got,
So I guess you're both the worst <u>AND</u> the best!
If you cross your T's and all your I's you dot,
The process of elimination,
Will weed out all the rest!
And that's the real test.
A bird in the hand, is worth two in the nest!"

And that's the way that Halloween went!
And that's how those few
precious days were spent,
In love with each other,
Dad, Mom, Sister and Brother,
And in love with laughter,
And the joys of life,
And a Lord like no other!

So,
Donny and Autumn shared,

"*Little Rip*"

As it began to sleet and snow!

The Angel with the golden hair,
and
The Ghost with little feet,

On a Halloween night, a long,
Time ago.

The End

<u>**Author's Note:**</u> The events which prompted and inspired this Halloween story occurred over 40 years ago. And yet, we still don't know what <u>Autumn Claire's Plan</u> was…to get herself a kitten! In fact, it is my hope, that our story ended on such a satisfying note that you didn't even realize that her plan was neither implemented nor revealed; but, it <u>was</u> realized…even to some extent against her will. I also hope you will note that something more important was indeed revealed:

> *For we know that God works <u>all things</u> together for good for those who love the Lord, for those who are called according to God's purpose.* Romans 8:28, Author's paraphrase.

Now, someone is bound to say, *"Well, empirical evidence and the facts certainly don't support that view! There are just too many things that happen which are NOT good! Therefore ALL things DON'T work out like that verse promises!"* Let me answer that seemingly undeniable fact:

Perhaps my dearest friend and fellow student in the Ph.D. program at The Southern Baptist Theological Seminary in Louisville Kentucky, was Molly Marshall-Green, known now for many years as Dr. Molly Marshall. She was, until March 1, 2020, President of Central Baptist Theological Seminary, located in Kansas City Kansas. Shirley, Autumn, Donny and I, drove to hear Molly preach one Sunday years ago (somewhere beyond Lexington Kentucky) when she and I were still working toward our Ph.D.'s in Louisville. I'm sure Molly has forgotten it, but I never shall. She took as her text that day, Romans 8:28 and broke down the Greek and the sentence structure and here's what she found:

<u>The proper rendering of that classic text is:</u>
> *For we know that God is at work in all things, <u>with our cooperation</u>, for good in all things to those who love the Lord and are the called-out ones, according to God's purpose!*

Therefore, (And this is the present author, and not Dr. Marshall, but I think she would agree.) <u>God's Perfect Will</u> desires that ALL things work out for good in our lives; but, <u>His Permissive Will,</u> permits us to live with our foolish choices. Freedom of choice (Freewill) is one of the Bible's most clearly and consistently stated doctrines. There is ALWAYS a degree of difference between <u>God's Perfect</u> Will and our <u>Stubborn Will!</u>

So ultimately, what's the difference? God wills nothing but goodness in our lives…so what's the problem? <u>You and I are part of the equation!</u> <u>THAT IS THE PROBLEM!</u> But, God will go right on working in our lives to will and to do His good pleasure in our lives….and in all things….and that promise will follow us all the days of our lives. Why? Because He has a Hope and a Plan for our lives, for good and not for evil.

You will recall that Autumn always insisted that to get a kitten, according to her plan, would take two! There was no other way. She was right! But she had the wrong two. *All it takes is the Lord and You!*

The following pages are Photos of Dr. Don Claybrook Sr's four children and his only granddaughter! Listed from the first-born to the last-born! Unless otherwise noted, all the photos are by Don Claybrook, Sr. and Don Claybrook, Jr.

1. Landa Patrice (Claybrook) Boutte

2. Autumn Claire (Claybrook) Kriofske

3. Donald Adrian Claybrook, Jr.

4. Liberty Jackson (Jack Claybrook) Reyes

5. Don Claybrook Jr.'s and my *daughter-in-law* Becky's daughter and my only granddaughter, Abigail Ivie Claybrook (all grown up), shown here in her high school cap and gown.

June 4, 2018
7:00 PM

44

Autumn Claire (Claybrook) Kriofske all grown up!

Photo credit: Whyland Studio, Jeffersonville Indiana, 1985

Donald Adrian (Donny) Claybrook, Jr. all grown up!
And my only granddaughter, Abigail Ivie Claybrook

Landa Patrice (Claybrook) Boutte

Landa Patrice (Claybrook) Boutte

Donald Adrian (Donny) Claybrook, Jr.   **Autumn Claire (Claybrook) Kriofske**

Liberty Jackson "Jack" Claybrook-Reyes

Liberty Jackson "Jack" Claybrook-Reyes

Donny and Autumn Claire Claybrook

Landa Patrice, all grown up
(With Dad who gave her away!) Don Claybrook, Sr.
Photo credit T.L. Johns, the bride's uncle.
All Photos by Don Claybrook, Sr. *unless otherwise noted.*

CPSIA information can be obtained
at www.ICGtesting.com
Printed in the USA
BVHW020336300921
617804BV00014B/488

9 781665 537285